For Nicole

First published in the United States of America in October 2012
by Walker Publishing Company, Inc., a division of Bloomsbury Publishing, Inc.
www.bloomsburykids.com

For information about permission to reproduce selections from this book, write to
Permissions, Walker BFYR, 175 Fifth Avenue, New York, New York 10010

Library of Congress Cataloging-in-Publication Data
Yoon, Salina.
Penguin and Pinecone / written and illustrated by Salina Yoon.
    p.   cm.
Summary: Penguin and Pinecone form an unlikely friendship, even when they must live far apart.
ISBN 978-0-8027-2843-2 (hardcover) • ISBN 978-0-8027-2844-9 (reinforced)
[1. Penguins—Fiction. 2. Pine cones—Fiction. 3. Friendship—Fiction.] I. Title. II. Title: Penguin and Pine Cone.
PZ7.Y817Pg 2012   [E]—dc23   2011037221

Art created digitally using Adobe Photoshop
Typeset in Maiandra
Book design by Nicole Gastonguay

Printed in China by Hung Hing Printing (China) Co., Ltd., Shenzhen, Guangdong
1 3 5 7 9 10 8 6 4 2 (hardcover)
1 3 5 7 9 10 8 6 4 2 (reinforced)

Penguin and Pinecone

a friendship story

Salina Yoon

 Walker & Company

One day, Penguin found
a curious object.

It was . . .

. . . too brown to be a snowball

. . . too hard to be food

. . . and too prickly to be an egg.

"Whatever you are, you're COLD!"

Penguin got busy.

Penguin loved his new friend.

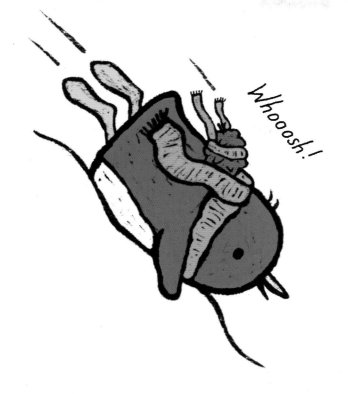

Whooosh!

Wheee!

achoOO!

Uh-oh . . .

"What's wrong with my friend?"

"It's too cold here," said Grandpa. "Pinecone belongs in the forest far, far away. He can't grow big and strong on the ice."

Penguin sighed. "I'd better take you home, Pinecone."

Penguin packed his sled for
the long journey.

The wind pushed hard . . .

. . . but Penguin pulled harder.

Finally . . .

"The forest! Pinecone . . .
you're HOME!"

Penguin made a cozy
nest out of the softest pine
needles he could find.

The day grew hotter and hotter.

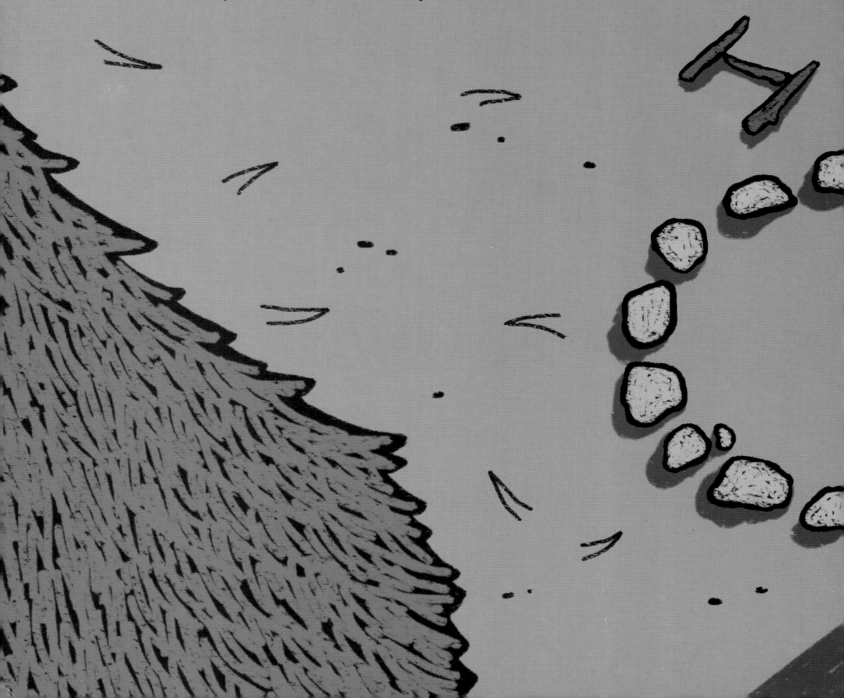

"Good-bye, Pinecone. You will always be in my heart."

Time passed . . .

and passed . . .

and passed.

Had Pinecone grown big and *strong* like Penguin had?

Penguin set off to find out.

"PINECONE!"

Penguin and Pinecone played and played.

Pinecone was sad to see Penguin go,
but the forest is no place for a penguin.

Penguin and Pinecone may
have been far apart,

but they always stayed
in each other's hearts.

When you give love . . .

. . . it grows.